THE SLITHEEN

501 316 282

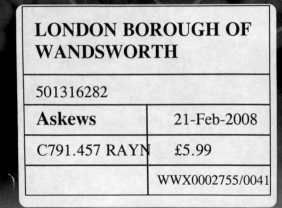

BBC CHILDREN'S BOOKS
Published by the Penguin Group
Penguin Books Ltd, 80 Strand, London, WC2R 0RL, England
Penguin Group (USA), Inc., 375 Hudson Street, New York, New York 10014, USA
Penguin Books (Australia) Ltd, 250 Camberwell Road, Camberwell, Victoria 3124, Australia.
(A division of Pearson Australia Group Pty Ltd)
Canada, India, New Zealand, South Africa.
Published by BBC Children's Books, 2006
Text and design © Children's Character Books, 2006. Written by Jacqueline Rayner.
Images © BBC 2004
10 9 8 7 6 5 4
Doctor Who logo © BBC 2004. TARDIS image © BBC 1963. Dalek image © BBC/Terry Nation 1963.
BBC logo ™ & © BBC 1996. Licensed by BBC Worldwide Limited.
DOCTOR WHO, TARDIS and DALEK and the DOCTOR WHO, TARDIS and DALEK logos
are trade marks of the British Broadcasting Corporation and are used under licence.
Printed in China.
ISBN-13: 978-1-40590-247-2

CONTENTS

The Slitheen may have baby-like faces, but they're certainly not cute! Slitheens love the thrill of the chase and will happily hunt down humans and with their enormous claws and pointed teeth, humans don't stand much of a chance against them.

'Slitheen' isn't the name of an alien race, it's the surname of a family of alien criminals who come from the planet Raxacoricofallapatorius. The Slitheen are on the run from their home planet, where they have been sentenced to death for their criminal activities. Now they roam through space, looking for ways to make a profit and they don't care who they hurt along the way.

To remain undetected, a Slitheen disguises itself by using a compression field to squash down its giant form until it's small enough to fit inside a bodysuit made from the skin of a murdered human. Unfortunately a lot of the mass is converted into gas, which then escapes with an unpleasant noise and a nasty smell of decaying carbon. That's one way to detect a disguised Slitheen! Another is to look for the telltale zip across its forehead.

Name:	The Slitheen family
Close relations:	The Blathereen family, the Rackateen family
Height:	approx. 2.44m (8')
Skin:	Green
Eyes:	Black
Weakness:	Acetic acid (vinegar)
Home planet:	Raxacoricofallapatorius
Species:	Raxacoricofallapatorian
Profession:	Criminals

Nearly two and a half metres tall

Excellent sense of smell helps to track prey

Scarily sharp teeth

Threatened female can exhale poison through her mouth, from her lungs

Compression field controller

Fearsome claws

Body made of living calcium

Threatened female can manufacture and shoot a poison dart from within her finger

TEST YOUR
KNOWLEDGE

Members of the Slitheen family are scattered across the galaxy, all looking for ways to make money and survive while on the run from the other Raxacoricofallapatorians and the fearsome Wrarth Warriors, the police of their star system. One branch of the family, led by Jocrassa Fel Fotch Pasameer-Day Slitheen, moved into the fuel-supply business, and came to Earth...

Jocrassa Fel Fotch Pasameer-Day Slitheen disguised himself as Joseph Green, MP for Hartley Dale (who became Acting Prime Minister). He tried to persuade the United Nations to give him the nuclear access codes.

Sip Fel Fotch Pasameer-Day Slitheen disguised himself as Assistant Police Commissioner Strickland and attempted to kill Jackie Tyler and Mickey Smith.

Another Slitheen disguised himself first as Oliver Charles, Transport Liaison, then as General Asquith.

Other Slitheen disguised themselves as Group Captain Tennant James of the Royal Air Force, Ewan McAllister, Deputy Secretary for the Scottish Assembly and Sylvia Dillane, Director of the North Sea Boating Club.

BLON FEL FOTCH PASAMEER-DAY SLITHEEN

Blon Fel Fotch disguised herself as Margaret Blaine of MI5, and was the only Slitheen to escape from 10 Downing Street. Still disguised, she became Lord Mayor of Cardiff, and set up the Blaidd Drwg (Welsh for 'Bad Wolf') Project in an attempt to get a nuclear power station built in the city.

Nearly everyone who stood in her way died mysteriously and painfully, but she showed a rare compassionate side to her nature when she let a pregnant journalist go free.

THE BLATHEREEN

The Slitheen's greatest rivals are their cousins, the Blathereen. Each side is forever trying to get the better of the other with their dodgy business deals. It was the Blathereen who forced the Slitheen out of their fuel business by undercutting prices.

Blathereen disguises in the year 2501 are more impressive than those their cousins used 500 years earlier. They can fit into the skins of humans of any size, and have small vertical zips on the top of their heads, which are easy to hide. The Doctor and Rose encountered a number of Blathereen on the penal colony Justicia, under the control of the Blathereen Patriarch, Don Arco.

TEST YOUR KNOWLEDGE

THE DOCTOR AND ROSE

The Doctor and Rose managed to thwart both the Slitheen's plan to turn the Earth into starship fuel, and Blon Fel Fotch's plan to escape the planet by causing a nuclear explosion in Cardiff's time/space rift.

Although the Doctor later became friendly with two Slitheen who were fellow prisoners on Justicia, it's fair to say that the Doctor and Rose will never be favourites of the Slitheen family.

JACKIE TYLER

Rose's mum, Jackie, was terrified when she discovered that the policeman who was interviewing her was really an alien. But when the Doctor told her how to defeat the monster, Jackie put aside her fear to create one big vinegary mixture containing gherkins, pickled onions and pickled eggs. resulting in Sip Fel Fotch exploding messily, and Jackie becoming the first human to kill a Slitheen.

MICKEY SMITH

Rose's boyfriend Mickey played a big part in defeating the Slitheen invasion of Downing Street. With the Doctor's help, Mickey hacked into the Royal Navy's computer systems, and launched a missile from submarine *HMS Taurean* which he guided towards 10 Downing Street. The Slitheen were destroyed along with the building, thanks to Mickey.

The Doctor, Rose and Harriet Jones survived, safe inside the steel walls of the Cabinet Room.

HARRIET JONES

Harriet Jones, MP for Flydale North, was the first person to discover that the Slitheen had infiltrated Downing Street. She helped the Doctor and Rose to fight the monsters, and convinced the Doctor that he had to carry out his plan to blow up the building and wipe out the Slitheen — whatever the cost.

Her part in the Slitheen defeat helped Harriet become Prime Minister of Great Britain and while she's running the country, it would be a brave Slitheen who dared to set foot there again.

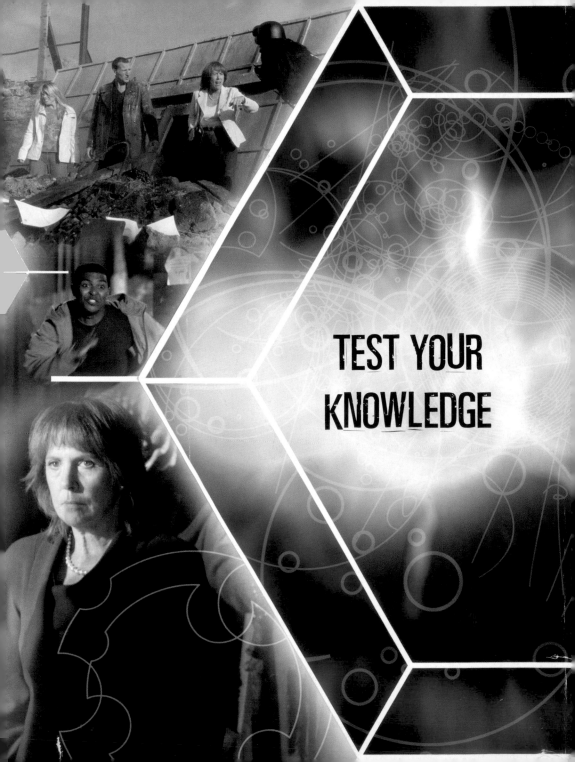

TEST YOUR KNOWLEDGE

RAXACORICOFALLAPATORIUS

The planet Raxacoricofallapatorius is a beautiful place — not the sort of world you'd associate with criminals like the Slitheen. In fact most Raxacoricofallapatorians are peaceful and law-abiding. Raxacoricofallapatorians hatch from eggs, which are kept in hatcheries. Adult Raxacoricofallapatorians sleep in nests.

Most children are taught mathematics and poetry, except the Slitheen children, who are taught to hunt and kill. The Slitheen have declared that one day they will return home and claim this paradise for themselves!

EXECUTION

The Slitheen have been sentenced to death, which means that any member of the family who returns to Raxacoricofallapatorius faces a painful public execution. First a thin acetic acid is prepared. Then the criminal is lowered into the Cauldron of Atonement and boiled. The acetic acid eats away at the skin until it is all gone, after which the internal organs fall into the solution. Gradually the Slitheen is turned into soup while he's still alive. Finally the soup is drunk by Raxacoricofallapatorian officials.

Needless to say, the Slitheen will do anything possible to prevent being sent back to their home planet. For now.

THE SLITHEEN'S WEAKNESS

When Jackie and Mickey were attacked by a Slitheen, the Doctor had to think fast to save them. He needed to know the Slitheen's weakness and he found it. As the Slitheen are made out of living calcium, which would be weakened by their compression field, they could be destroyed by a mild solution of acetic acid, such as vinegar.

Harriet Jones likened the Doctor's plan to that of Hannibal. Hannibal was a Carthaginian general who crossed the Alps with a large army (and 40 elephants!) in 218BC. A historian called Livy tells how Hannibal cleared a path through the mountains by heating the rocks that were in his way with fire, and then pouring vinegar over them so they dissolved.

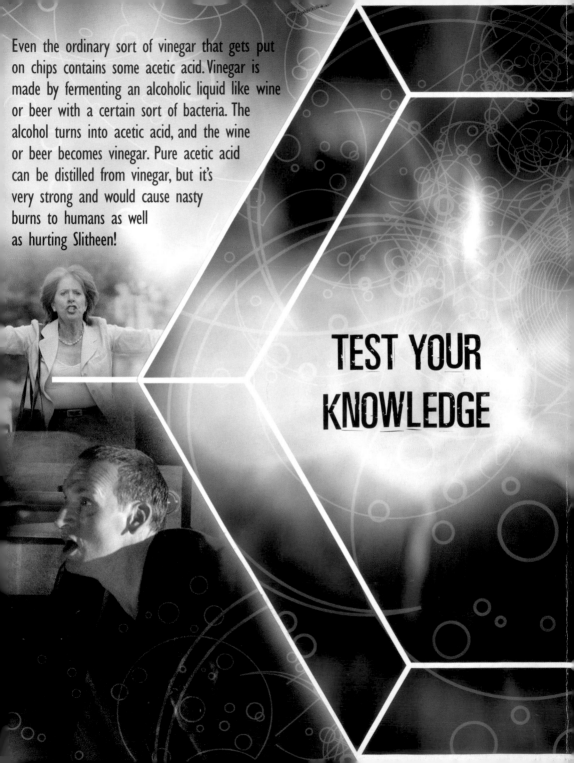

Even the ordinary sort of vinegar that gets put on chips contains some acetic acid. Vinegar is made by fermenting an alcoholic liquid like wine or beer with a certain sort of bacteria. The alcohol turns into acetic acid, and the wine or beer becomes vinegar. Pure acetic acid can be distilled from vinegar, but it's very strong and would cause nasty burns to humans as well as hurting Slitheen!

TEST YOUR KNOWLEDGE

COMPRESSION FIELD

The Slitheen wear devices around their necks which enable them to control a compression field. The compression field allows them to shrink their bodies enough to fit inside a human skin. When a Slitheen is released from the compression field, a bright blue light surrounds it.

The neck device also establishes a connection between Slitheen. When the Slitheen used electrified identity cards to kill a roomful of alien experts, the Doctor turned the tables by inserting a card into Jocrassa Fel Fotch's neck device, and all the Slitheen were electrocuted.

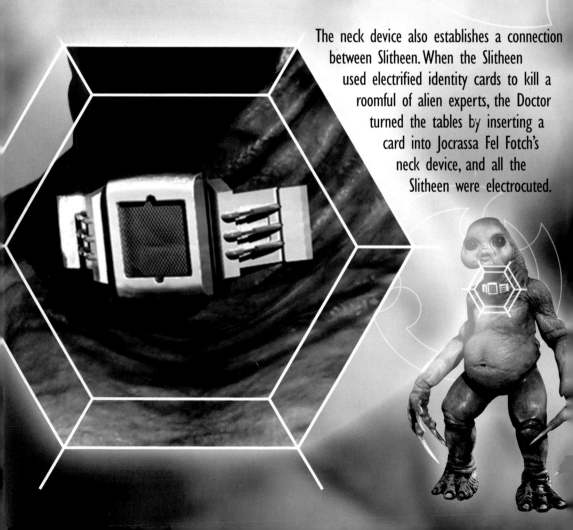

TELEPORTATION

Blon Fel Fotch used an emergency one-person teleport to escape from the exploding 10 Downing Street, but unfortunately for her, without coordinates, she ended up in a skip on the Isle of Dogs.

She was better organised when the Doctor came looking for her in Cardiff, using the teleport device (its components disguised as a brooch and a pair of earrings) to get away — but each time she tried it, the Doctor used his sonic screwdriver to reverse the teleport and bring her back, so eventually she gave up.

SPACESHIPS AND SPACE PIGS

Humans were astonished when a spaceship careered through the London sky and crashed into the Thames, especially when it destroyed Big Ben along the way! But the Doctor realised the ship was a decoy. It had been launched from Earth, done a slingshot manoeuvre around the planet and come back down to Earth again.

Inside this ship was an Earth pig that the Slitheen had adapted to make it appear alien. Its brain was wired up and it was made to walk upright and wear a spacesuit. The pig was taken to Albion Hospital to be examined, but the scared creature was shot by a soldier when it tried to run away. The Slitheen also had their own spaceship, complete with slipstream engine, parked in the Thames.

THE EXTRAPOLATOR

Blon Fel Fotch built a nuclear power station on top of the space-time rift in Cardiff. The planet would explode, but she had a stolen alien device, a tribophysical waveform macro-kinetic extrapolator, to keep her safe. Not only would it protect her with a force field, it would enable her to ride the power waves to take her off the planet and out of the solar system, just like a pan-dimensional surfboard.

The Doctor foiled that plan, but didn't realise what would happen next. The extrapolator locked on to the TARDIS and began to open the rift using the ship's power supply. However Blon hadn't reckoned with what would happen when she started to pull the TARDIS apart...

TEST YOUR KNOWLEDGE

THE SLITHEEN'S PLAN

After landing on Earth, the Slitheen began attempting to infiltrate the British Government. When a satellite detected a Slitheen signal under the North Sea, a decoy ship and alien pilot was sent up to act as a diversion from the real Slitheen ship. But that wasn't all it did. Having killed the Prime Minster, the Slitheen were now able to assemble all the Earth's top alien experts together in one place. They thought they had come to Downing Street to discuss the new alien threat, but every expert except the Doctor was killed by the Slitheen.

The evidence of the ship and the death of the alien experts could then be used to persuade the United Nations to release the nuclear codes to the disguised Slitheen, who would use them to start World War Three and destroy the planet. Then they planned to sit back and wait for customers to turn up to buy their advertised starship fuel, made from the molten, radioactive chunks of the Earth. If only the Doctor hadn't turned up just in time to foil their plans!

BLON'S SECOND CHANCE

Arriving in Cardiff, the Doctor, Rose, Mickey and Captain Jack were surprised to see a photo of the new Lord Mayor — Margaret Blaine, aka Blon Fel Fotch Pasameer-Day Slitheen. The Doctor decided to take Blon back to Raxacoricofallapatorius, where she would be executed.

Blon tried to persuade him that she regretted her past and had changed, but this didn't seem likely when she revealed her intention of using the power of the TARDIS to destroy Earth so she could escape from the planet.

However when she looked into the heart of the TARDIS, she was transformed into an egg. Perhaps the TARDIS realised she really did want to change, and was giving her the chance to start again.

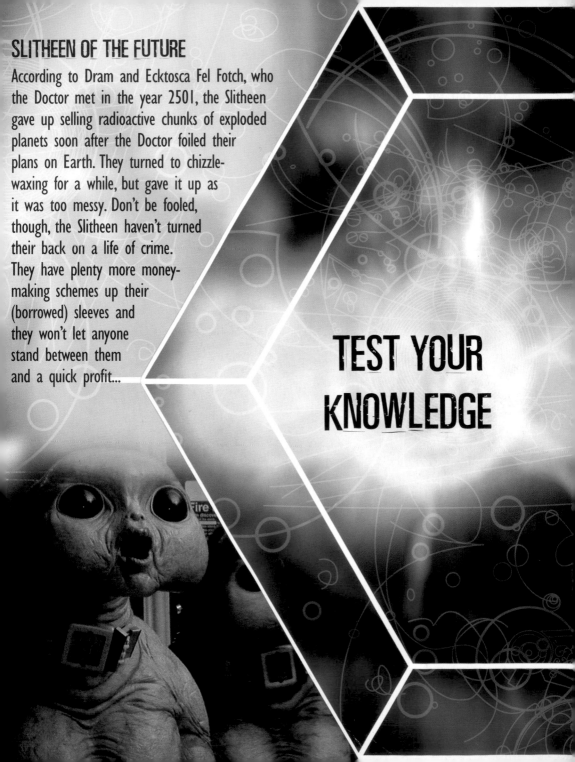

SLITHEEN OF THE FUTURE

According to Dram and Ecktosca Fel Fotch, who the Doctor met in the year 2501, the Slitheen gave up selling radioactive chunks of exploded planets soon after the Doctor foiled their plans on Earth. They turned to chizzle-waxing for a while, but gave it up as it was too messy. Don't be fooled, though, the Slitheen haven't turned their back on a life of crime. They have plenty more money-making schemes up their (borrowed) sleeves and they won't let anyone stand between them and a quick profit...

TEST YOUR KNOWLEDGE

ANSWERS

Meet the Slitheen
1(b) 2(a) 3(c) 4(b) 5(a)

We Are Family
1(a) 2(c) 3(a) 4(c) 5(a)

Human Enemies
1(c) 2(c) 3(a) 4(c) 5(b)

Background
1(c) 2(b) 3(b) 4(a) 5(a)

Transport and Technology
1(b) 2(a) 3(b) 4(b) 5(c)

Adventures with the Slitheen
1(b) 2(c) 3(b) 4(b) 5(a)

NO FUN AT THE FAIR

NO FUN AT THE FAIR

"Ahhh!" breathed the Doctor, flinging his arms wide and nearly hitting Rose in the face with his candyfloss. "A fun fair. What better way could there be of spending a summer Saturday?"

Rose grinned. She would have preferred the beach, or even the shops, but the Doctor was having so much fun she wasn't going to ruin things by saying so.

"Now, just time for one more ride..." the Doctor span on the spot and ended up pointing at the fair's star attraction, the giant twisty-turny water slide. "Oh yes."

"Oh no," said Rose. "Not after hot dogs, chips, ice cream and candyfloss."

"Time Lord digestion!" the Doctor protested.

"Human digestion!" Rose pointed out, gesturing at her stomach. His face fell, and she couldn't help laughing. "OK, you go and get soaked, I'll look for something a bit quieter."

The Doctor hurried off, and Rose looked around. They'd done the merry-go-round, the dodgems and the test-your-weight machine; the ring toss, the duck hook and the coconut shies. A sign caught her eye – a vampire with enormous fangs was beckoning her towards the ghost train. She shrugged. Why not? Not a chance a few plastic skeletons would scare her after the things she'd seen, but it might be a laugh.

She bought a ticket and took a seat. It was the end of

the day and there were only a couple of other people on the ride – well, that might make it a bit creepier.

With a jolt, they were off. Rose tried to get into the swing of it, giving half-hearted shrieks as fake cobwebs brushed her face and mummies lurched unconvincingly towards her.

And then she screamed for real.

There in the shadows as the car jolted round a corner was a monster. Green baby face, staring black eyes, terrifying claws.

A Slitheen.

Rose wrenched at her seat belt. The fastening clicked open and she climbed up on the seat. "Sit down in front!" yelled an angry man from the car behind, but she didn't care. She peered back into the darkness, desperately trying to catch another glimpse of the Raxacoricofallapatorian and then Rose blinked as she found herself outside again. While her back was turned, the car had pushed through the final barrier and the ride was over.

She jumped out and made her way back to the exit. "Oi!" cried a voice as she went to push through the barrier. A hand grabbed her arm and she turned to see a burly, moustached man wearing a 'ghost train' baseball cap.

Rose shook off his hand. "I've got to get back in there," she said.

He pointed at a sign above the exit. No Entry.

She sighed. "Right. OK. I'll go in the other way, then." She ran back round to the front of the ride.

"One, please," she said, holding out a pound coin to the ticket collector.

He shook his head. "Sorry, we're just closing."

This was impossible! She ran to the ride's entrance,

just as the doors were slammed shut. And locked.

She screamed again as a hand clapped down on her shoulder. But it belonged to a soggy but happy-looking Doctor. "You're a bit jumpy," he said. "I prescribe a toffee apple. You missed a treat, you know. You've got to try that water slide…"

"I saw a Slitheen!" Rose gasped.

"You what?"

"A Slitheen! In there!" She gestured towards the ghost train. "Big, green, scary…"

"Sure it wasn't Frankenstein's Monster? Or your mum in a mood?"

She gave him a hard stare. "Yes. I'm sure." She suddenly had a thought. "The ghost train guy! He was huge! No wonder he wouldn't let me back in. Come on!"

She ran back to the train exit, the Doctor jogging

behind. The moustached man was cleaning down the cars. Rose stalked up to him and stood there with her hands on her hips. "Aha!"

"Oh, you again," the man said. "Look, you're not going in, all right?"

"Not all right," said Rose, sticking out a finger to prod his stomach. "Feeling a bit gassy, huh?"

The man doubled over. "What on Earth do you think you're doing?"

"The question is, 'What d'you think you're doing on Earth?'" She yanked off his baseball cap, to reveal... his head. A totally hair-free and zip-free head. "Oh," she said.

"Do excuse my young friend," said the Doctor, joining them. "She's upset at missing the water slide." He led the red-faced Rose away.

"Look, I didn't imagine it," she insisted. "I saw a Slitheen."

"Then we wait till everyone's gone and look for it."

It was a while before the coast was clear. The Doctor got out his sonic screwdriver, but before he could tackle the lock they heard sounds from within the ghost train. Heavy footsteps. Rose and the Doctor hid as the door opened from the inside – and the sinister baby face of a Slitheen peered out.

"Blimey," the Doctor whispered. "You were right." They held back as it set off across the fairground. "Right," said the Doctor. "I'm going to check out the ghost train, see there aren't any more of them. You keep an eye on that one. But don't get too close!"

Rose nodded, and hurried off. What sinister things might the Slitheen be getting up to? She watched, nervous, as it... had a go at the ring toss.

The Slitheen's huge claws weren't made for precision, and the rings fell short. Undeterred, it moved on to the test-your-strength booth. There the hammer thumped down and the tinny ring of the winner's bell rang out. The Slitheen raised its arms in victory, and went on to the next attraction. Rose felt a stab of pity as the giant monster failed to fit into a dodgem car. Pity – for a Slitheen? But this Slitheen wasn't rampaging and killing. It was just trying to have a bit of fun. Could it be stranded on Earth? Forced to hide during the day in the one place it could blend in – a display of freaks and horror-film faces? Perhaps it wasn't even a Slitheen, but one of the good Raxacoricofallapatorians. She had to find out – perhaps they could help it.

Distracted, she lost track of the creature for a moment.

No, there it was, coming out of a trailer. That was odd, what had it wanted in there? Rose ducked inside to see. And gasped.

There was a big poster along one wall: *'Coming soon: Super Slitheen Space Spectacular!'* And everywhere there were plans and diagrams and research notes. Every stall or ride from the fair was represented – but in a hideous, twisted form. Shies with human heads instead of coconuts! A ring toss where people could be ringed instead of soft toys or cheap vases. Dodgem cars where the object was to ram into as many humans as possible. And scariest of all – the human hunt! The human was chased through the fair, ending with the *piece de resistance* – the human hunt water slide!

This Slitheen wasn't stranded. It was a scout. It was carrying out research for its own fair of fear.

And she'd felt sorry for it!

Rose went to the door. The sooner she found the Doctor, the better. The sooner she told him what she'd discovered about –

The Slitheen. There, in the doorway. Watching her.

"Little human girl!" it hissed, happily. "I caught the stench as I passed. How kind of you to volunteer to help with my research..."

Rose backed away. "Like I'm helping you with anything."

"Oh, but you must," the Slitheen told her, reaching out with a claw. "One little human girl, all alone – no one to notice us. No one to see as we test the human hunt..."

Rose stopped breathing for a split second. Then, before the Slitheen could react, she dashed forward, ducking under its outstretched arm and running as fast as she could.

The Slitheen was close behind her. She pelted onwards, desperate and scared. Couldn't quite believe she was outpacing the monster. Then she realised – it was deliberately staying just behind. Deliberately guiding her steps. This was part of the fun of the chase...

Where was the Doctor? Was he still in the ghost train? She hoped they would go there, but instead the Slitheen shepherded her into the Tunnel of Love. Ignoring the little swan-shaped boats, Rose half swam, half waded through, fighting her way through curtains of stars and love hearts. There was a click and a flash as she reached the exit, and the distraction made her stumble, but the Slitheen didn't want the chase to end just yet. Rose's stomach flipped to see where they were heading next – the water slide. The end of the hunt.

She scrambled up the steps, the Slitheen close behind

her. All she could do was try to keep as far ahead of the monster as possible, and hope that she'd think of something – or that the Doctor would turn up.

The Doctor! As she began hurtling downwards, she suddenly spotted a figure on the ground. "Help!" she yelled. But then she was inside a tube, whizzing round corner after corner, with no way of knowing if he'd heard. Perhaps the Slitheen would get stuck in the tube? No such luck. Rose was out in the open again – and so was the Slitheen.

She could see the Doctor! But why wasn't he racing to her rescue? He was just standing at the bottom of the slide – was he pouring something into the water?

She'd find out soon. Because this was the almost vertical drop to the pool – terrifying even if you didn't have a killer monster right behind you.

Rose hit the water. It winded her, and she couldn't move. Any second now the Slitheen would land on top of her...

Hang on. Something smelled like... chips?

The Slitheen landed in the pool, claws raised. "And now, little human girl, for the finale!" it cried – and then stopped.

Suddenly, without warning, the Slitheen exploded.

Hardly able to believe her luck, Rose crawled out of the pool. She was exhausted, she was soaking wet, and she was covered with gunky chunks of green Slitheen goo, but she was safe. Oh, and she smelled, too. Someone had put vinegar in the water...

The Doctor threw the last of the empty bottles on a pile, and gave Rose a hand to stand up. "Nicked it from the chip van," he said, as she linked her arm through his.

"There, told you should try the slide..."

Everything was OK now. The Doctor would make sure there'd be no Super Slitheen Space Spectacular, no human games or hunts.

"I got you a souvenir," he said, as they made their way back to the TARDIS. "You see, there's this screen outside the Tunnel of Love where they display the photos taken inside.

A Day to Remember

Admittedly I was a bit hurt you'd chosen to go in with someone else, but I got over it..."

He handed her a photo. There, inside an enormous red heart, was a picture of a soggy Rose while the terrifying Slitheen loomed threateningly above her. Underneath was written 'A Day to Remember'.

"Thanks," Rose said to the Doctor. "Otherwise I might forget. After all, it's not often that you have so much fun at the fair."

DOCTOR · WHO